Paul Hutchens

MOODY PRESS
CHICAGO

Revised Edition, 1998

Original Title: *Adventures in an Indian Cemetery*

ISBN: 0-8024-7017-3

1 3 5 7 9 10 8 6 4 2

Printed in the United States of America

PREFACE

Hi—from a member of the Sugar Creek Gang!

It's just that I don't know which one I am. When I was good, I was Little Jim. When I did bad things—well, sometimes I was Bill Collins or even mischievous Poetry.

You see, I am the daughter of Paul Hutchens, and I spent many an hour listening to him read his manuscript as far as he had written it that particular day. I went along to the north woods of Minnesota, to Colorado, and to the various other places he would go to find something different for the Gang to do.

Now the years have passed—more than fifty, actually. My father is in heaven, but the Gang goes on. All thirty-six books are still in print and now are being updated for today's readers with input from my five children, who also span the decades from the '50s to the '70s.

The real Sugar Creek is in Indiana, and my father and his six brothers were the original Gang. But the idea of the books and their ministry were and are the Lord's. It is He who keeps the Gang going.

PAULINE HUTCHENS WILSON

1

There were two very important things I didn't have time to tell you about in my last story, *Screams in the Night*. One of those two things was what happened when we ran *ker-smack* into the kidnapper himself and had a terrible fight with him, and the other was a strange moonlight adventure in an Indian graveyard.

In fact, the two were sort of mixed up together. The kidnapper was doing something mysterious in that Indian graveyard, and some of the gang accidentally stumbled onto him. Did you ever see an Indian cemetery, the kind the Chippewa Indians have away up in northern Minnesota? That's the country where the Sugar Creek Gang was spending its awfully fast vacation. Those cemeteries are the strangest-looking places in the world. I'll tell you about the one we had our adventure in just as soon as I get to it.

I was sitting on the farther end of the long dock with my back to the shore, swinging my bare feet. I was holding onto my fishing rod and watching the red-and-white bobber way out in the lazy water.

Now and then the bobber would bob a little and move around in a small, lazy circle on the surface of the big blue lake, which meant that the live minnow I had put on the hook for bait was down there in the water somewhere and was still frisky enough to be a very attractive afternoon lunch for any hungry bass or walleye or northern pike that might be dumb enough to come along and eat it.

I'd been sitting there for maybe ten minutes, not getting any bites except from deer-flies, which had terribly sharp stings. So I smeared some insect repellent on my bare hands and arms and face and legs and feet and was getting a good tan to take back home with me after vacation would be over.

It was about three o'clock, and all the gang except me were in their tents taking an afternoon nap, which was what we all had to do every day. A boy feels so good on a camping trip that he might get too tired, and when a boy gets too tired without enough rest and sleep, he can get sick easier or catch cold, and his body will be a good growing place for most any kind of germ.

I'd already had a short nap and had sneaked out by myself to the end of the dock, put a frisky, wiggling chub on for bait, and cast my line way out into the deep water. I was hoping that by the time it was time for the gang to wake up, I'd be getting a terribly big fish on my line. Then I could yell and scream, and we'd all have a lot of excited noise to start the rest of the afternoon off right.

After that, there'd be a picture to take of the fish and me, and maybe it would be big enough to enter in the northern Minnesota fish contest. And then maybe our hometown paper, *The Sugar Creek Times,* would publish the picture, and the write-up would say something like this:

> SUGAR CREEK BOY
> LANDS FOURTEEN POUNDER
>
> Bill Collins, eleven-year-old son of Theodore Collins, who lives just three and one-half miles west of here, has distinguished himself to anglers by landing a fighting, wild-running, very fierce-looking northern pike at Pass Lake, Minnesota, where he and his pals are camping.

I was still a little sleepy, and, since it's never very good fishing that time of day anyway, I sort of nodded. I must have dozed off, because all of a sudden I felt the dock shaking a little behind me, and looking around I saw one of the gang coming, his fishing rod in his hand and his straw hat flapping. His round face was grinning, although he had the finger of one hand up to his lips, meaning for me to keep still.

"Hi, Poetry!" I whispered.

He stopped close to me and looked down into my freckled face and said, "Hi, Bill! *Sh!* Listen! I've just thought of something important."

I watched him wiggle-twist his pudgy fingers into his khaki shirt pocket and pull out a piece of white cloth with something wrapped up in it.

"What you got?" I said.

And he said, "See this piece of glass we found up there beside the sandy road last night where the kidnapper's car was stuck?"

I remembered all about it—the kidnapper's car stuck in the sand, the wheels spinning, him swearing and swearing, and Poetry and I hiding behind some bushes watching and listening, not knowing till afterward that a little kidnapped girl was in the backseat of the car right that minute.

The man all of a sudden had climbed out of the car and let out some of the air of his back tires to increase traction and then had climbed in again and roared away. After he'd gone, our flashlights had shown us something bright, and Poetry had picked it up and kept it, saying it was a clue. But it was only a broken piece of glass.

I stared at the piece of thin glass in Poetry's hand and thought of how it was curved like a piece of broken bottle.

"He was maybe drinking," I said, "and threw the bottle away and it broke and—"

"It's *not* a piece of broken bottle," Poetry said. He lifted the minnow pail that was sitting beside me and put it behind him so he could set himself down beside me. Then he said, "Take a look *through* it. It's a piece of lens from somebody's glasses, and I'll bet the kidnapper broke them while he was having trouble getting his car out of the sand. Or maybe the little Ostberg girl wiggled and twisted, trying to get away, and they broke that way."

Poetry made me look through it, which I did, as he held it so that it wouldn't get dropped. While I was looking through it, I noticed it magnified things and also brought things up closer.

And then I saw my red-and-white bobber start moving faster than a four-inch-long minnow could have pulled it. Out—out—out it went. Then it dunked under, and the line on my rod tightened, and *then* the ratchet of my reel started to sing. As quick as a flash I tightened my grip on the pole and my thumb on the reel, letting the line unwind, waiting for the fish—or whatever was on the other end of the line—to get the minnow swallowed.

I quick dodged my face away from Poetry's hand and the piece of glass and got set to sock the line. I gave a quick fierce jerk, and you should have seen what happened.

Away out there about fifty feet, there was a fierce boiling of the surface of the water and a wild tugging on my line. I heard the reel spinning and felt the line burning hot on my thumb. I was sure I'd hooked a terrific northern pike, and Poetry and I all of a sudden started making a lot of fishermen's noise.

I scrambled to my feet and didn't even bother to notice what was going on behind me. I heard Poetry trying to get out of my way and out of the way of the minnow pail, which he was having a hard time doing, but I couldn't look back to see. I had to hold onto my fish. I did hear Poetry grunt five or six quick grunts, though, and heard the pail get itself knocked over and heard and felt a heavy body go *ker-whamety-thump* on the dock.

Then there was a noisy splash beside me, and I knew it was the minnow pail. It'd had about twenty-five live chubs in it and shouldn't have been left on the dock in the first place but should have been down in the fresh water to keep the minnows alive.

Then there was another splash. I took a sideways look and saw Poetry himself down there in the water.

He grabbed the pail, yelling, "The lid wasn't fastened, and the minnows are all spilled out!" Poetry held up the empty pail with every single minnow gone that Barry, our camp director, was supposed to fish with that evening.

Well, my heart would have been beating hard with being to blame for losing the minnows if it wasn't already beating terribly fast with excitement because of the fish on my line. It was no time to worry over spilled minnows, though. So I yelled down to Poetry, "Look—look!"

And when Poetry looked, he saw what I saw. A great two-foot-long fish of some kind I'd never seen before jumped out of the water, showed every bit of himself in a long leap, and then splashed back in again and dived straight to the bottom.

And then all the gang were waking up in their tents. They came running out to the end of the dock to help by yelling and telling me what to do and what not to do all at the same time.

Splash! Zip! Swish!

I tell you it was an exciting time there for a few noisy minutes, with one member of the gang after another bounding onto the dock, and all of them telling me what to do and what not to do and why, and also how to and how not to.

But soon I had that big fish coming in a little closer to the edge of the dock where I was. Then, because he may have felt the way a boy would feel if he saw some giants yelling and waving their arms, he'd get scared and make a fierce run for the deep water again. And every time, I'd let him run and let the hot line go sizzling under my thumb from the whirring reel, so as not to let him break the line.

In about five minutes the fish was up close enough for Big Jim, the leader of our gang, to reach out with a long wooden-handled dip net and get him into it. In another jiffy he was landed.

"It–it–it's a *dogfish!*" Dragonfly, the pop-eyed member of our gang, yelled when he saw the lunging, fierce-looking, large-mouthed fish in Big Jim's net. I looked at Dragonfly's eyes, which, when he's excited, get extra large the way a dragonfly's eyes are.

"It is not," Circus said, squinting at it and at the same time shading his eyes with his hand to keep the sun out of them. Circus, being our acrobat, felt so good after his afternoon nap that he started walking toward the shore on his hands. He wound up in the shallow water beside the dock, because he accidentally lost his balance and fell off in a sprawling splash right beside Poetry, who was already there.

Little Jim, the greatest little guy in the gang and the most innocent-faced one of us, squeezed his way through to where I was and said, "It's a two-foot-long bullhead!"

"It can't be," red-haired Tom Till said, squinting his blue eyes at the fish. "Bullheads have horns, and there isn't a one on him!"

Well, it turned out that Dragonfly was right —it *was* a terribly big dogfish and wouldn't be good to eat, although some people might want to eat it.

Anyway, that's how the minnow pail with Barry's two dozen minnows got turned over and all the minnows spilled out, and why Barry, for a friendly sort of punishment, decided that Poetry and I had to go to a resort about a quarter of a mile up the lake and get more minnows.

And that's how Poetry and I ran *ker-smack* into the kidnapper mystery again. This is the way it happened.

2

When Poetry and I realized that we had to take a hike up the lake to a resort on the other side, all of a sudden the weather seemed terribly hot, much too hot for two boys to have to hike so far to get a pail of minnows. In fact, it wouldn't be good for the minnows to stay in the pail all the way back without changing the water, the same as it is not good for boys not to have fresh air. All fish need plenty of oxygen.

"I'm sorry, boys," Barry said, his one all-gold front tooth shining in the sunlight, "but there'll be plenty of time. And besides, wasn't there a rule about the afternoon rest period lasting until a certain time? And didn't two boys break that rule? What do you say, gang?" He whirled around and asked Big Jim and Little Jim and Little Tom Till and Circus and Dragonfly.

Not a one of the gang answered at first, on account of all of us were very loyal to the rest of us, and nobody wanted anybody to be punished.

Then Dragonfly spoke up and said, "I think it's a good idea if I can go along with them."

He looked wistfully at my freckled face, then at Barry, just as Poetry said, "We could save time, and wouldn't have to stop on the way back to change the water on the minnows, if we could take the boat and the outboard motor."

The very thought sent a thrill up and down my spine. If there is anything I'd rather do than anything else, it is to sit in the stern of a boat with the steering handle of an outboard motor in my left hand and feel the vibrating rubber grip on the handle and hear the motor's roar. I like the feel of the wind in my face, too, as the boat shoots out across the water with its sharp prow making a V-shaped path and with water spraying over the gunwale and spattering a little on my freckled face.

Boy, oh boy! If Barry would only let us! It would be wonderful if the minnows could be brought back in just maybe five minutes after they were put in the pail!

Barry looked from one to the other of us—at Poetry's round, mischievous face, at my freckled and maybe excited face, and at Dragonfly's thin face with his dragonflylike eyes. I noticed that Dragonfly's eyes were squinting at things as if he had eyestrain and needed glasses. Then he sneezed and pulled out his big red handkerchief to stop the second and third sneezes by squeezing his nose shut and pressing hard against his upper lip at the same time.

Barry looked at Dragonfly and said to the three of us, "I believe there are a lot of wildflowers along the shore, and you boys might stir up a lot of extra pollen walking, and that'd be hard on Dragonfly's hay fever, so—well, go ahead, you three!"

Whew! I was glad we'd spilled the minnows!

Little Jim piped up and said, "It'd be hard

on my hay fever to have to walk too if I *had* the hay fever. And if I had to be punished, *I'd* rather go in the boat too!"

Barry grinned at Little Jim and said, "All right, if you think you can stand the punishment."

Little Jim said he could.

Pretty soon we were ready to go after the minnows. Now I hardly noticed the hot weather, even though right that minute the sky was like a big, upside-down, all-blue breakfast-food bowl that had a big round yellow hole in its bottom. Through that yellow hole a lot of fierce heat was pouring down on us and on the blue lake and all over the Paul Bunyan Playground, which was what people called that part of the North where we were. Paul Bunyan was an imaginary big lumberman who used to live up North. It was imaginary Paul Bunyan's imaginary big blue ox, Babe, whose imaginary footprints formed all the big lakes in Minnesota.

Dragonfly, Poetry, Little Jim, and I were just ready to shove off and go roaring out across the lake when Big Jim yelled to us from the shore and said, "Wait a minute!" which we did. He came hurrying out to the end of the dock to where we were.

"You forgot the roll call."

I was surprised, because we were going to be gone only thirty minutes maybe. I'd forgotten that that was one of Barry's rules. He'd given us a list of things that he said were "standard" for anybody in a boat, and the whole gang had been memorizing the list. And here I was, forgetting it the very first day all on account of wanting to get going in a hurry. Every time any of us went out in the boat somebody "called the roll" to see if we had all of our equipment.

Big Jim looked at a slip of paper he had in his hand, which showed he wasn't trusting his memory either, and read off the list of things for us, and we answered. It reminded me of our teacher at Sugar Creek School calling the roll of his seventeen pupils and we answering our names if we were there.

"Fire extinguisher!" Big Jim read.

Dragonfly said, "Present," and held up an empty tin can, trying to be funny and giggling to make it sound funny, which it didn't, but Dragonfly's giggle did. There was a fire extinguisher on one of the big boats we used, but none of the small boats had any. The fire extinguisher was in case the outboard motor caught fire. It wouldn't be any fun if you were far out on a big lake and your motor and boat caught fire and your boat burned out from under you.

"Extra gasoline!" Big Jim called from his slip of paper.

And Little Jim answered by tapping with his stick on the two-gallon red gasoline can in the bottom of the boat. Little Jim always took his stick with him wherever he went.

"Screwdriver, pliers, and wrench!" Big Jim yelled.

Poetry opened Barry's tackle box, and there, right in the top drawer, were all three.

"What do we need pliers for?" Dragonfly asked me, he being the kind of person who always wants to know all the whys of everything.

"To take the hooks out of the big fish we catch," Poetry said, and Dragonfly said in a complaining voice, "Let's get started—we aren't going fishing."

"An extra spark plug!" Big Jim went on calling the roll, and I noticed that the spark plug was also there in the first drawer in a plastic bag.

"Oars!" Big Jim said.

We didn't have any.

Poetry said, "Don't need 'em. We've got plenty of gasoline and a good motor."

"Oars!" Big Jim said again, louder. "Go get 'em! They're in Barry's tent!"

Poetry, who nearly always had a hard time having his mind changed for him, scowled but knew that scowling wouldn't help. So up he stood, and out he stepped, and pretty soon back he puffed with two long green oars. He shoved them under our boat seats, where they'd be safe and wouldn't fall out easily.

Big Jim went on. "Life vests or safety cushions for each person on board!"

There were only three cushions in the boat and four boys, so Dragonfly had to chase back to the tent for another one.

"An extra length of starter cord," Big Jim said.

We had to have that too, on account of one might break or get dropped in the water while we were away out in the lake, and who would want to row back?

"Hurry up!" I called to Big Jim on the dock. "We're in a hurry!" I was just itching to get out there on the lake and feel the boat doing what I wanted it to. If there is anything any boy likes, it is to run something that will do what he wants it to do when he wants it to, which is maybe why my dad and mom feel good when I do what they want me to, I thought—which was a crazy time to think it.

And for a second I felt a wave of homesickness go swishing over me like a big wave of water, and I wondered what my folks were doing at Sugar Creek and how my baby sister, Charlotte Ann, was standing the heat. And I wished Mom could have a chance to come to a lake like this and get cooled off—only it was hot here too today. I could imagine her sitting in this pretty green-and-white boat with Charlotte Ann and Dad and with me steering and roaring fast out across the blue water.

Dragonfly came dashing back with a red safety cushion.

Big Jim stooped over and unwound the starter cord, which I had already coiled around the starter disk of the motor so as to be ready to give a quick sharp pull the very second we were out in deep water.

"You can't go with that starter cord!" Big Jim said and held it up.

"Hey!" I said. "Let me have it. We're in a hurry!"

"Oh no, you're not!" Big Jim argued. He pulled out of his pocket a round piece of wood about five inches long and quick made a special knot in the end of the starter cord and tied the cord to the middle of the stick.

"There you are," he said. "Now if anything happens and this cord falls into the water, it will float, with this piece of wood tied to the end to hold it up."

Well, that was the end of the roll call, and in a minute we were off, just as Big Jim called to us to hurry back because we were all going to visit an Indian cemetery before supper.

"I don't see any sense in taking all those things along every time we go out," Dragonfly complained, and I agreed with him until a little later.

It was a great ride and felt just as I thought it would, and I wished it could have lasted a long time. Soon, though, we rounded a bend in the lake and started zipping along the shore toward the resort where we were to get the minnows. Straight ahead of me, I could see a neat little rustic log cabin, which most of us saw at the same time and started talking about.

"There's Santa's cabin," Little Jim said. "Look! He's painted his boathouse green!"

Santa, you know, was the big man who had invited us to come North in the first place to camp on his property.

"Yeah," Poetry yelled above the sound of

the motor, "he's painted the inside green and white both—we saw it last night. That's where the kidnapper had the little Ostberg girl."

That started me thinking of the exciting time Poetry and I had had last night.

We took turns yelling to Little Jim and Dragonfly all the different things that had happened—how Poetry and I had got up in the middle of the night and with our flashlights had sneaked out of our tent and down to the boathouse, because earlier last evening we thought we'd heard something inside.

"You know what I wish?" Poetry yelled to me.

I yelled back, "What?"

"I wish we'd got a good look at his face so we could maybe help the police find him. He's pretty sure to be hiding out up here somewhere."

"I wish I had been with you last night," Little Jim said. His small, mouselike, innocent face had a tense look on it, and he was gripping the stick in his hand so tight the knuckles showed white.

"What'd you have done?" Dragonfly, who was sitting in the prow of the boat, yelled to him.

And Little Jim said, "I'd have socked him with this stick."

I looked at him and, remembering how he loved everybody and didn't like to see anything or anybody get hurt, I was surprised.

But then he said in one of the fiercest voices I'd ever heard him use, "Anybody that'd treat a helpless little girl like that ought to be socked."

Dragonfly said, "Aw, you wouldn't hurt a fly."

Little Jim got a set look on his face, gripped his stick tighter in one hand and the side of the boat with the other, and said, "I say I'd have socked him!" He raised his stick and whammed it down on the gunwale right close to where Dragonfly was sitting.

"Hey!" Dragonfly yelled, "I'm no kidnapper!"

We steered close to Santa's dock, then I swerved the boat so that we went swishing past and started a lot of rolling waves toward his shore. Then we zipped on up the shoreline toward the resort where we were going to get the minnows for Barry.

I noticed that Poetry had his hand on the pocket of his khaki shirt where his clue was—the piece of lens that we both had decided was from somebody's broken glasses.

Dragonfly, who had been looking toward the green-painted boathouse, asked, "How'd you know the little Ostberg girl was in that boathouse?"

"'Cause we found a girl's scarf up there where the kidnapper's car was stuck in the sand, and it had fresh green paint and white paint on it."

We were nearly there. We steered toward the dock of the resort, not knowing that we were about to have another experience that would start us to thinking even harder about the kidnapper.

3

The minute the resort owner saw our boat coming toward his long dock, he stood up from where he'd been sitting in the shade of an oak tree and came wobbling out to the dock to meet us, waving his arm to let me know on which side of the dock he wanted us to put our boat.

"He wants us on the opposite side from which the wind blows," Poetry said.

As I shoved the steering handle in the right direction, the green-and-white boat swerved in a wide curve, and we came gliding up right to where we were supposed to—almost.

I was coming in pretty fast, not realizing maybe how fast we'd been coming.

"Cut the motor off!" Poetry yelled to me.

I did, quickly shoving the speed control lever to the left as far as it would go. I was trying to tilt the whole motor forward quick, the way you're supposed to when you're coming into shallow water and don't want the propeller to strike the bottom, which wouldn't be good for it and which a good boatman never lets it do.

The lake must have been more shallow right there than I realized, because even before it had happened I realized it was going to, and it was too late. My hand on the steering handle felt what was happening at the same time I heard it, and I knew my propeller down there in the water had struck the bottom of the lake before I had shut off the motor.

I quick tilted the motor forward far enough to lift the propeller off the bottom and out of the water too, just as the prow, where Dragonfly was sitting, struck the sandy shore instead of the dock.

Dragonfly yelled, "For land's sake! Watch where you're going!"

"For the *land's* sake, is right," Poetry yelled, trying to be funny.

"Watch what you're doing!" Little Jim yelled to Dragonfly, just as Dragonfly stood up.

As the boat struck the sandy beach, Dragonfly lost his balance and tumbled forward and sideways. He landed half in the water and half out. The parts of him *not* getting wet in the very shallow water were his hands, head, and shoulders, and also his feet, which were up in the air.

Dragonfly sneezed, as he always does when he smells anything he is allergic to and also most any other time. But he was a good sport. He squished himself out of the water, grinned, and said to all of us, "The water's fine." Then he pulled his wet bandana out of his wet hip pocket and wiped his face with it.

"What can I do for you boys?" the resort owner said to us.

We told him, and pretty soon we were all out of the boat watching him get the minnows for us. He kept them in a big cement tank filled with running water. It was in an open pavilion with only a roof over the tank, so there would be shade and lots of air.

I never saw so many minnows in my life. It was fun watching the resort owner dip a long wooden-handled net into the tank and scoop up several dozen different kinds and carefully pick out the chubs, letting them slip into our minnow pail. Chubs were the kind Barry wanted.

Just as the man was counting out the last five or six minnows, Little Jim, who was squeezed in between Poetry and me, with Dragonfly on my other side, all of a sudden looked up from watching the wiggling, squirming, slippery minnows in the net and said, "There's somebody else coming for minnows."

I looked where he was looking and saw what he saw. A big white boat with a powerful outboard motor propelling it was coming toward the dock.

The stranger acted as if he knew exactly how to run a motorboat. He swerved around the end of the long dock, shut off his motor right away, tilted it forward to save the propeller from striking the bottom, and in almost no time was standing up, wrapping his anchor rope around one of the dock posts, and climbing out.

He didn't want any minnows but some gasoline instead. He called up to us and said, "I see you've got gasoline drums up there against the garage. I'd like to have some for my boat."

"Sure!" the resort man called. "Take your

can over and help yourself! Be through here in a minute!"

In a minute we were finished. Poetry paid for the minnows, and the four of us followed the footpath down to the dock.

On the way, Poetry whispered to me and said, "He's wearing dark glasses."

And I said, "What of it? I wish I had some. That sun has a terrible glare to it."

"*Sh!*" Poetry said in a mysterious whisper, which somehow sent a scared feeling through me, and I knew what he meant.

Right away my mind was as alive as a pailful of minnows, with all kinds of ideas leaping and wiggling and slithering over each other—some of the ideas getting all tangled up with a lot of other ideas.

I always hated to have Poetry think of things first, though, so I said again, "Dark glasses? What of it?"

"What of *what?*" Dragonfly asked.

And I said, "The man up there getting gasoline for his motorboat is wearing dark glasses."

"What of it?" said Dragonfly. "I'll bet they're restful to his eyes. I'll bet if I had a pair I wouldn't have so much eyestrain and wouldn't sneeze so much."

"Whyn't you buy a pair?" Little Jim asked.

Then I remembered that Dragonfly's folks didn't have much money and that a real *good* pair of dark glasses, if they had ground lenses, maybe would cost a lot.

Before we got to our boat, the man with the

dark glasses had his can filled and was hurrying back down to his own boat, which he'd tied to the dock post.

Since our boat had been beached, instead of docked, it took us a little while to get it *un*beached. But the stranger was in his boat right away, rowing out a little to where it would be safe to start his motor without the propeller's striking on the bottom.

"Let me run the boat back," Poetry said. And as soon as he could, he stepped in and sat his big self down in the stern like a king on a throne.

Little Jim was last to get in. Then he spoke up in a commanding voice, which sounded funny for him, and said, "Hold it! Wait for the roll call!"

"We've *had* it!" Dragonfly said. "Get in and let's get going. I want to see that Indian graveyard."

Pretty soon we were all in. Little Jim and I grabbed the oars and started rowing us out toward deep water. Poetry had the starter rope coiled around the starter disk and was waiting to give the rope a sharp pull as soon as we were out far enough.

I was glad to be sitting beside Little Jim, because for some reason he was a very likeable little guy. I liked the way he handled his oar. It also felt good to tell him how to do it and have him believe me and do exactly what I told him to and do it exactly right.

Just then there was a roar, and I looked out

beyond the dock to where the man with the dark glasses was. He'd started his motor, and his boat was vrooming away real fast.

"I wish we could have a boat race," Poetry said. "I'll bet our boat could outrun his."

"Don't you dare try it!" I said.

Little Jim piped up and said, "If it was a terribly long race, and we had to have our gas tank filled a lot of times, I'll bet we'd lose. We only got a two-gallon can, and he just bought five gallons."

Dragonfly, trying to be funny and not being, said, "But our can's new, and his is an old battered up one with nearly all the paint off it."

Little Jim, also feeling mischievous, said, "But his shirt had more paint on it than ours do."

For some reason I jumped as if I was shot when he said that. "What?" I said.

And Little Jim said, "Yeah, his shirt had green paint on its right sleeve."

Poetry looked at me, and I looked sort of waveringly into his bluish eyes, and I knew he and I were thinking the same thing.

I said to Poetry, "We're out far enough. Give her a whirl. Let's see if we can catch up with him and see if there's any white paint on his shirt too." I held my forefinger up to my lips to let him know I was thinking about the kidnapper who'd been in Santa's boathouse last night.

Poetry already had the gasoline shutoff

valve open as far as it would turn, and the air vent open, and the speed control lever pushed over to the place where it said "Start."

When I said, "Give her a whirl," Poetry quickly got set, with his right hand on the five-inch-long piece of wood Big Jim had tied on the end of the starter cord, and gave a quick sharp pull. And just like a boy ought to get out of bed in the early morning when his dad calls him, that motor leaped into noisy life and let out a terrific roar, and we were off.

That is, we thought we were. The motor was running terribly fast, and Poetry was pushing the steering handle around so the boat would turn and we could go racing after the man in the other boat to see where he went and if he had green and white paint on his shirt.

But we weren't moving. We were just sitting still out there. In fact, we were drifting toward the dock and the shallow water again. Also, right that second a little breeze whisked across the lake, and our boat swung around sideways. And in spite of the motor's whirring fiercely, and Poetry's shoving the steering handle this way and that, nothing happened!

What on earth! I wondered, and so said we all, only each of us used different words. And all the time the man in the big white boat was roaring up the lake to a place where, pretty soon, his boat would round the bend in the shore and he would disappear.

Poetry looked at me and I at him, and he

said to me, "You broke a sheer pin back there when you didn't stop the motor soon enough and tilt it forward soon enough to keep it from hitting bottom."

I knew it was true and that, even though the motor was racing like a house afire, the little propeller down there in the water wasn't even moving.

"You mean we'll have to *row* back?" I asked.

"We will." Poetry shoved the speed control lever to the left as far as it would go and shut off the air vent and the gasoline shutoff valve. And that's how come we were very glad Big Jim had called the roll and made us put the oars in the boat.

"It's a great punishment for spilling minnows," Little Jim said, grinning and grunting at the same time, as he and I sat beside each other, pulling away on our two oars while Dragonfly and Poetry rode free.

"Poetry ought to have to help." Dragonfly spoke up from behind Little Jim and me. "He broke the rest hour rules the same as Bill did."

Little Jim and I sat facing Poetry, who, as you know, was in the stern in front of us where the motor was. Poetry and I kept our eyes looking straight into each other's. We both knew we were thinking the same thing—that the man with the dark glasses, whose boat right that very minute was rounding the bend in the shore, was maybe the kidnapper of the little Ostberg girl.

Poetry spoke up then and asked all of us,

"Did any of you guys notice whether the boat had any name on it?"

None of us had noticed any name, which meant maybe there hadn't been any. If there had been, it might mean that the boat belonged to some resort, and most resort owners had their boats all named the same name as their resort and also had a number beside the resort name, so as to identify the boat.

"I'll bet it was his own boat," Little Jim said.

"Privately owned, anyway," Poetry said with a puckered forehead. "He probably stole it."

Little Jim scowled at that, because he never liked to think anybody was bad until he found out for sure he was.

We rowed along. Little Jim and I pulled steadily toward the bend in the lake. When we got there, it'd be Dragonfly's and Poetry's turn to row.

"Who said I had to row?" Dragonfly asked.

I looked back over my shoulder and saw him lean his skinny self back and raise his spindly legs and put his feet up on the sides of the boat and yawn.

Then he said, "It's wonderful to breathe all this fresh air and not have to sneeze," which it was, but right that minute he sneezed.

Maybe it was because he had leaned back and had looked up toward the sun and that had maybe made tears in his eyes, some of which had started down on the inside of his nose and had tickled him and made him sneeze.

"You need dark glasses," I said to Dragonfly.

That reminded Poetry of one of the 101 poems that he knew by heart and was always quoting, and it was:

> Once a trap was baited with a piece of cheese,
> It tickled so a little mouse, it almost made him sneeze;
> An old rat said, "There's danger, be careful where you go."
> "Nonsense," said the other. "I don't think you know."
>
> So he walked in boldly, nobody in sight,
> First, he took a nibble, then he took a bite;
> Snap the trap together, close as quick as a wink,
> Catching mousey fast there, 'cause he didn't think.

I'd learned that poem last year, and I liked it.

"Dragonfly's the mouse that got caught," I said.

And Poetry said, "This boat was the mouse-trap, and a free fast ride was the cheese he bit on, and the oars are the jaws of the trap."

Little Jim said with a grin in his voice, "Who was the old rat that said, 'Danger, be careful where you go'?"

"Hey!" Dragonfly yelled out all of a sudden, "Be careful where *you* go!"

At the same second I felt leaves swishing

across the back of my red head, and right away we were in the shade of an overhanging tree along the shore.

It was a good place to change oarsmen. Since Poetry was too heavy to sit side by side with anybody as light as Dragonfly—then the boat wouldn't be balanced right—we decided to let him row by himself. Little Jim and I sat where Poetry had been, and Dragonfly stayed where he was.

The rest of the way to our dock and camp, Poetry and I kept looking each other in the eyes. I knew that as soon as we got to shore, he would have a secret to tell me, and that it would be something very important he had thought up about the kidnapper and how to catch him.

The gang was there on the dock, waiting and yelling and razzing us because we had to row back, and wanting to know why. Circus, who had been practicing the loon call, kept calling over and over again to us in a long, trembling high-pitched wail that sounded even more like a loon than a loon does.

Everybody was in a hurry to get started to the Indian graveyard when Barry, who was in his tent, came out with some letters in his hand, which he'd been writing. He said, "Any of you boys have any letters or cards to send to your folks? I'll have to run these into town right away if they are to make the late afternoon train."

He looked around at different ones of us

and acted surprised when nearly all of us, even little red-haired Tom Till, had written cards or letters to our folks—even *Dragonfly,* whose handwriting was terrible and who hated to write anything he didn't have to.

When Barry took our letters, I noticed that Big Jim gave him two letters to mail. I managed to be real close to Barry when Big Jim handed the letters to him, and one of the envelopes was a sort of pinkish color, and I knew it wasn't written to his *parents*. I knew also whom it was written to. She was maybe one of the nicest girls in all the Sugar Creek territory and was our minister's daughter, whose name was Sylvia.

Right away Big Jim had his back turned to Barry and was whistling a mixed-up tune of some kind. He had a stick in his hand and was stooped over, poking it into the ashes of our dead fire, where we'd cooked our dinner that day.

The fire was dead because we'd put it out. It's not safe to leave any fire anywhere in any woods. In fact, it's against the law to even start one in some places, or the whole dry forest might catch fire and burn up thousands of dollars' worth of timber and people's houses and wild animals and everything.

For some reason I got a stick real quick and helped Big Jim poke around in the dead ashes, because I had also handed Barry two letters, and *one* of them had been to my parents.

"You boys are on your own for a while," Barry said. "I'll meet you at the cemetery. Just follow the old sandy road from Santa's cabin up the hill and past the fire warden's house, and you can't miss it. About a half mile up that road you'll come to an opening on the right side, and there you are."

Then Barry was gone in the station wagon, which is what we'd all come up North on our vacation in, and we were left alone, which is what we wanted anyway. It is ten times more fun to have fun when you are alone with your gang than when a grown-up person is with you, doing what is called "supervising" your play.

Of course, we all liked Barry plenty, but a gang needs to be by itself part of the time if it wants its fun to be fun.

In minutes we would all be tumbling along together toward Santa's cabin, past the boathouse, where Poetry and I had heard strange noises the night before, and on up the hill to where the kidnapper's car had been stuck in the sand, and where Poetry found the piece of broken glass.

Then we'd go past the fire warden's house, where, I remembered, the police had made a plaster of paris cast of the kidnapper's tire tracks. And then we would hike on the rest of the way, following the same sandy road the kidnapper had followed last night till we came to the Indian cemetery.

There we'd look around at the tombstones and see the different things and tell ghost stories and maybe pick some ripe raspberries—there might not be any raspberries, but then there might be, I thought. The graveyard we sometimes had our gang meetings in at Sugar Creek was full of weeds and had sumac and blue vervain and wild roses and wild raspberries and, earlier in the year, wild strawberries. And sometimes we'd find a bumblebees' nest and fight the bees and kill them and get a lot of honey.

Boy oh boy! It felt good to be all alone with nobody except just the gang.

"We'll have a gang meeting in the cemetery," Big Jim said. "There's something very important to vote on. Remember, school is going to start in about two weeks after we get home again."

"School!"

Nearly all of us yelled at Big Jim at the same time. What did he want to spoil our vacation for—reminding us of school?

And then we were on the way, running and jumping and playing leapfrog and laughing and having fun. I noticed that Big Jim had his pocketknife in his hand and was looking at the different trees as we went past. For some reason I had mine out too and was helping Big Jim look for a beech tree, which is the kind of tree you carve anybody's initials on.

We didn't find any, though, but we did walk past and through what seemed like a whole forest of white birch. But it was against good campers' etiquette to spoil the whitish, silvery bark on a birch tree, so we didn't stop to carve anybody's initials.

Every now and then Circus would let out a loony loon call, and Dragonfly would sneeze, and Little Jim would sock something with his stick, and Poetry would start a poem and be shushed up by some of us. We all liked Poetry, but we didn't like poetry the way he did.

All the gang knew about Big Jim's thinking our minister's daughter was almost the nicest girl in the whole Sugar Creek territory. She was pretty and polite and studied hard and could throw a snowball as straight and as hard as any boy. She was also an honest-to-goodness Christian and wasn't ashamed of it and acted as if she'd rather be a real one than be the queen of anybody's country.

I kept on helping Big Jim try to find a beech tree—and was wondering how long it would take me to grow a little black fuzz on my upper lip like Big Jim had on his, and wishing I would hurry up and grow as big as he was.

Pretty soon Big Jim stopped and looked at a pretty silvery white birch tree's bark, and I knew he was wishing it wasn't against good woodsmen's etiquette to carve initials on white birch trees.

Little Jim had been walking along close to Big Jim and me as though maybe he was looking for a beech tree himself. But I knew he wasn't —not because he wanted to carve anybody's initials on one, anyway. He was awfully smart, though, that little brown-haired guy, and sometimes he got a mischievous streak, which surprised everybody because he was almost always kind of serious.

He had a mischievous grin on his small face right that second, and I guessed he was thinking of something. Sure enough, he was.

He stopped beside Big Jim and me and looked at the silver bark of the birch tree and said in Big Jim's direction, "It's a very pretty bark, isn't it? It's all *Sylvia* colored!"

Then he gave a terrific whack with his stick at a cylinder-shaped brown cattail that grew right close by and was off on the run to where the rest of the gang were, up ahead of us. His short legs pumped like a small boy's on a tricycle, and his brown curls shone in the sunlight like the brown flowers at the top of a long cattail stalk.

4

On the way to the Indian cemetery we had a lot of different kinds of excited talk, mostly about the kidnapper. Poetry and I showed the rest of the gang the place out in the woods where we'd found the little girl the night before, wrapped in an Indian blanket.

Then we stopped at the fire warden's gate, where the police had made a plaster of paris cast of the tire tracks. The friendly fire warden came out of his cabin and told us he was glad to see us again. We had been to see him the night before.

And then we went on up the old sandy road toward where the Indian cemetery was supposed to be.

"Where do you suppose the kidnapper is now?" Dragonfly wanted to know.

Little Tom Till said, "Maybe a million miles away, spending all the ransom money the little girl's daddy gave him."

I didn't think he was a million miles away, and neither did Poetry. He squeezed my arm, and I knew what he was thinking.

Pretty soon, our winding, twisting snakelike road, which had a lot of surprise turns in it as it wound its way through the trees, came to a little open place, and Dragonfly said, "Look!

There's some farmer living up here. See all those chicken coops?"

I looked where he was looking, and off to the side of the road in an open space were what looked to be twenty or maybe thirty weather-beaten, unpainted, very small houses about two or three feet high. But there wasn't any farmer's house—or barn or horses or cows or chickens or ducks or geese or sheep or children playing.

"It's the Indian cemetery," Big Jim said.

"What?" Little Tom Till asked. "Where are the tombstones?"

I was thinking the same thing myself. I'd been wondering what kind of gravestones there would be and what would be chiseled on them. I guess I'd been imagining it was like the graveyard at the top of Bumblebee Hill at Sugar Creek.

The little houses were used instead of tombstones, he told us.

Dragonfly had a very weird look on his face. He was the only one of the gang who was more afraid than any of the rest of us when we were in a graveyard, because his mother is superstitious and believes in ghosts.

We stopped in front of a rather new chicken-coop-looking house, and Dragonfly said, "It's awful spooky here. Let's get out."

"Can't," Big Jim said. "We have to have a meeting here."

"We have to wait for Barry," Circus said. "He's going to explain about Indian funeral rites and why they use little houses like these and stuff." Circus was looking at the long row of small houses all facing the same way, and I knew him so well, and what a good athlete he was, that I imagined he was thinking that those little houses would make good hurdles for him to hurdle over in a race.

"What are the little holes in the front of the houses for?" Dragonfly wanted to know.

Poetry, who did more reading than any of us, had read about that in a book, so he said, "That's to let the Indian's spirit go in and out. And also, the live Indians bring food and different things and leave it on the little shelf there in front of the hole for the spirit to reach out and get it. They come in the evening sometimes to bring any kind of thing to eat that the dead Indian used to like when he was alive."

Well, it certainly was an interesting place to be. We walked around, waiting for Barry.

And then Big Jim said we'd better have a meeting, which we started to have way up at the other end of the cemetery behind some sumac shrubs in some long mashed-down bluegrass. We were on the other side of a very special grave, which was larger than the others and had a low wooden fence around it.

"They bury the medicine men in an enclosure like that," Poetry said.

We were lying down in different directions, getting ready for Big Jim to call the meeting to discuss something important and to vote on it.

"I think the idea's crazy—bringing food for the Indian's *spirit* to eat," Circus said, rolling over all of a sudden from having been on his back and sitting up and saying what he said.

"*Sh!*" Big Jim said. "There comes an Indian now. Quiet, everybody. Don't make a sound."

I looked in the direction of the cemetery entrance, and somebody was coming. It was a man with black hair hanging down on his shoulders, with a feather stuck in it, but wearing ordinary people's clothes like most Indians up there wore. I got the strangest feeling. It was a half-scared and half-curious feeling, but it was a different kind of scared feeling than I'd ever had before.

He had a small brand-new-looking Indian basket in one hand like the kind we'd seen along the road on our trip up here, which the Indians were selling in their open-air roadside stores.

"He's coming this way." Big Jim shushed us with a very quiet but very firm shush, and we shushed quick.

Yes sir, he was coming our way, shuffling along with his brownish face very sober and looking around as if he was scared there might be an Indian ghost around somewhere.

I could hear all of us breathing now as we lay there. Little Jim, I noticed, had his hand on his stick real tight. Big Jim's face was set, and his jaws were working the way they do when he's thinking and wondering about something. And his eyes were squinted as he watched through the foliage of the sumac that was between us and the Indian.

Dragonfly was blinking and swallowing and had his handkerchief up to his nose and was stopping what might have been a whole flock of noisy sneezes.

I noticed something weird about Poetry, though. His forehead was puckered, and he was writing something in his notebook, which would probably be something he'd use to write a paper on when school started two or three weeks from now.

Just that second, Poetry's hand reached out and touched mine, and he pointed toward the Indian with the new basket in his hand.

"He's pushing something through the little hole," Poetry whispered in my right ear.

The man was squatted down, taking things —I couldn't see what—out of his basket and pushing them through the hole of the grave house in the little fenced-in enclosure, which Poetry had told us was the grave of a medicine man.

A second later, the Indian stood, looked around as if he was still scared of somebody's spirit watching him, and then hurried back toward the exit of the graveyard, where he ducked behind a tree and began to whistle a strange tune. He was soon out of sight and far enough away not to be heard.

"That was a very interesting tune," Poetry said.

Little Jim, who takes piano lessons and whose mom is the Sugar Creek church pianist, was lying on his back with his two hands up in the air making his fingers move as if he was playing the piano.

"What're you doing that for?" Little Tom Till wanted to know.

And Little Jim said, "I'm playing the music for the song he whistled, trying to think what it was, and I can't."

5

We were still all sprawled out in different directions in that old Indian cemetery, wondering, *What on earth?* because of what we'd just seen and heard, trying to explain things to ourselves.

I was watching Little Jim's puckered forehead and wondering whether he'd be able to think of the tune the Indian had been whistling. I knew that if anybody in the Sugar Creek Gang could think of it, he could, because his mom was not only the best pianist in the whole Sugar Creek territory but had a music library with two copies of nearly every hymnbook that ever was published. She also had copies of lots of music by nearly all the important composers.

Little Jim had to live in what my dad sometimes called "a musical atmosphere." So I knew if the tune the Indian had been whistling was any of the famous old songs, Little Jim would probably have heard his pretty mom play or sing it, and he might remember it.

But Circus, who has the best singing voice of any of us, remembered it first and said, "It's 'Old Black Joe.'"

Right away he started whistling it himself, and right away I remembered it, because we sometimes sang it for opening exercises in the Sugar Creek School.

"It might not be 'Old Black Joe,' though," Little Jim said. "It might be something else. Somebody wrote some church words to that tune once too. Mother sometimes sings it."

Then Poetry remembered it himself and started quoting some of the church words:

"Gone from my heart the world with all its
    charm.
Gone are my sins and all that would alarm.
Gone evermore, and by His grace I know
The precious blood of Jesus cleanses white
    as snow."

"I wonder which words he was thinking about," Little Tom Till wondered. "The church ones or the 'Old Black Joe' ones."

Big Jim answered, "It depends on whether he goes to church."

"There's an Indian mission church up here," I said, remembering one we'd seen last year. It was in an old railroad coach out in the forest.

"If he goes to church," Little Jim said, "then he might be a Christian. And if he is, then maybe he wouldn't stick anything in through a hole in somebody's grave house for the Indian's spirit to eat or smell—or maybe to look at, if it's something pretty."

That made good sense, I thought, but it also wrinkled up Poetry's forehead. He was still writing in his notebook, and it looked as though he was puzzled about something. I quick looked over his shoulder and saw this: "Might be a Christian Indian whistling a hymn. But if he was, then he wouldn't believe in making offerings to a dead Indian spirit. He might be an ordinary Indian, singing 'Old Black Joe,' which he learned somewhere."

"Wonder what he shoved through the little hole—something to eat, maybe?" I said.

"I'm hungry." Poetry closed his notebook and rolled over and sat up.

"Let's go look in and see," Tom Till suggested, and Dragonfly got a scared look on his face and said, "M–m–maybe the Indian's ghost has got whatever it was and ate it up."

We called a meeting, and we were just going to vote to decide whether to go and look in through the little hole, when all of a sudden we heard an outboard motor coming. Before I knew what I was going to do, I'd scrambled to my two kind of awkward feet and made a dive in the direction I thought the sound was coming from.

Most of the rest of the gang came after me.

I had to run only about fifty feet to get to where I could look down a little hill to the lake. And there I saw a big white motorboat plowing fast right straight toward the shore down below us.

In a flash Poetry, who had my binoculars, lifted them to his eyes and let out a low whistle.

"It's somebody in a white boat wearing a pair of dark glasses!"

"Boats don't wear dark glasses," Dragonfly said and sneezed.

"But dragonflies can sneeze," Poetry said, being only a little bit funny.

I could see with my bare eyes that Poetry was right. It was a man in a white boat all right, and he was heading straight toward our shore. Right away I remembered the man we'd seen earlier that afternoon, who had bought five gallons of gasoline at a resort on the other lake.

I sidled up close to Poetry and whispered to him, "How'd he get on this lake with that boat?"

Dragonfly must have guessed what we were thinking, since he had been with Poetry and me when we'd gone after the minnows. He said, "He came here on the Mississippi River."

I knew he was right. Anybody who knows anything about the country up where we were spending our vacation should know that the Mississippi River flows right through nearly all the lakes around where we were, and that a narrow channel of it leads from one lake to another.

"*Sh!*" Big Jim shushed us all and said quickly, "Quiet! All of you!"

We shushed.

It took the man with the dark glasses almost no time to bring the white boat up to shore, toss his anchor out, and wrap the anchor rope around a tree. Then he climbed out with a new-looking brown tackle box in one hand and made his way up the hill toward the cemetery. I noticed that in the boat was the five-gallon gasoline can, and for some reason I had the funny idea that we actually had, honest-to-goodness for sure, as plain as the nose on your face, run onto the trail of the kidnapper again.

We didn't dare let ourselves be seen, so we beat it back to where we'd been and flopped ourselves down on the grass behind the sumac again, panting and with hearts pounding, watching to see what the man was going to do.

He acted very strangely. He walked around in the graveyard as though he was half blind. Once he stumbled over a small grave and almost lost his balance as he came toward where we were, near the long grave house inside the fence.

Poetry, who was lying with his face close to my ear, whispered, "He acts like a half-blind man."

And Dragonfly, who was close to my other side, said, "Maybe he needs glasses."

I was sure that, whoever he was, he was the kidnapper. I wished the gang were near enough to make a dive for him in football style and get him down and sit on him until we could tie him up and call the police.

He just walked around through the cemetery as if he was somebody curiously looking around, the way people wander through other graveyards, reading the tombstones and thinking. But I noticed that all the time he was getting closer and closer to the medicine man's grave, where the Indian had stuck something inside a little while before.

I looked at Little Jim's face. It was tense, and the muscles of his jaws were working exactly like Big Jim's jaw muscles were. I also noticed he was crouched down as close to Big Jim as he could get.

You could have heard a pin drop, we were so quiet. The only noise was the swishing sound the man's shoes made as he walked, and the sad sighing noise that a very gentle wind was making in the boughs of the pine tree above the medicine man's grave house.

Just that second I saw a flash of something lemon yellow colored flit across from one chokecherry shrub to another, not far away. Then I heard a sweet song exactly like that a wild canary sings. There were a lot of wild canaries up where we were but not many other birds.

Even while I was all mixed up in my mind with a tangled-up mystery worrying me a little, I all of a sudden had a strange, good feeling sweep all over me.

It was the way I sometimes feel when I'm all by myself down along Sugar Creek and I hear birds singing all around in the trees, and one of the little riffles in the creek is bubbling cheerfully, and honeybees are droning in the old linden tree above the spring, and the heat waves are dancing above the wild rosebushes along the old rail fence that I'm maybe sitting on. It's a wonderful feeling, and makes you wish you had wings yourself so that *you* could fly. You're glad you're alive and feel that you and the One who made everything all around you are good friends. You're glad that everything you've ever done that's wrong has all been forgiven, and you wish all the people in all the world felt as you do.

When that pretty yellow canary flashed across that old Indian cemetery, I kind of wanted to fly *inside* again.

Then I heard the sound of a car coming up the road. I came down to earth and wondered if it was Barry and hoped it was. I also hoped it wasn't, because then the man might get scared and run away, and we wouldn't get to find out what he was doing.

The man must have heard the car too. He dropped down inside the fenced-in enclosure as if he had been shot, and you couldn't see anything of him.

It wasn't our station wagon though, because it had an old-fashioned noisy motor and it rattled on past. I could see a whirl of white dust rising above the shrubbery between us and the road.

Then the sound of the engine died out, and I saw the man's bare head rise above the low fence, then duck down again. And then the guy was squatted down in front of the long grave, looking in through the little spirit hole.

I looked at Dragonfly's dragonflylike eyes, and he was worried. I knew it was because his mother believed in ghosts. Little Jim had a half-afraid look on his face too, but I knew it wasn't for the same reason. He believed the same as his parents and also our pastor—that the very minute a Christian dies, his spirit goes straight to heaven and doesn't hang around anybody's graveyard. Besides, they don't get hungry or cold or need anything in heaven.

It's an odd feeling to have, though, when you're in a spooky graveyard with a lot of chicken-coop-shaped grave houses with holes in them like the holes Dad has in front of his beehives and you know that some people actually do believe in ghosts but shouldn't.

The next second the man was creeping away from the grave. The branches of the pine tree were very low right there, and he was stooped over to keep from getting his head bumped. He still had his fishing tackle box with him.

Then, just as if nothing had happened and he hadn't done anything strange, he started walking around among the grave houses again, working his way toward the outside of the cemetery. I knew he'd be going back to his boat within minutes and would be gone.

I just knew there was something in that tackle box, and I wondered if it was the ransom money for the little Ostberg girl. I wished I'd all of a sudden scramble to my feet and that all the gang would run like wild animals on a fierce stampede straight for the man and get him down, the way I'd wished we'd done before. But I felt so scared I was numb all over, and since Poetry and I were the only ones who maybe imagined he might be anybody suspicious, we didn't do a thing.

Then I heard another car coming and guessed that this time it *was* Barry's station wagon.

Quick as a flash, that man with the tackle box looked toward the entrance, made a kind of awkward dive straight for the other side of the cemetery, and disappeared over the edge of the hill.

Why on earth didn't we do something? I thought. *Why just lie here like a bunch of scared cats?* I'd started to get to my feet, when Big Jim reached out his hand and grabbed me and pulled me down hard, saying, "Don't move—not a one of you!"

I looked just in time to see our brown-and-yellow station wagon swing in at the other end of the cemetery. The minute its engine was shut off, I heard another motor start up down at the foot of the hill, and I knew it was the kidnapper, who had started his outboard motor and was about to roar away to safety. I just knew it!

What on earth! I thought again. Didn't Big Jim have any idea what was going on? Couldn't he think? I was half mad and was going to say something kind of fierce, when he said, "That was a wicked-looking gun he had in his pocket."

"Gun?" I said. "I didn't see any gun." But now I understood why Big Jim hadn't let us do anything. He'd seen the gun and knew it was more important—as my dad had also taught me —to have good sense than it was to be brave.

We all scrambled to our feet, just as Barry looked over to where we were and saw us and called, "Quick, boys! There's news on the radio about the kidnapper!"

As quick as seven flashes, all seven of us were untangling ourselves from ourselves, and tumbling over each other on our way to our feet, and then running fast toward Barry.

Poetry and I were together, because he and I had a secret we were sure the rest of the gang didn't know about. We were hurrying past the big pine tree whose swooping branches hung down over the medicine man's grave house, when Poetry stopped, stooped over, and scooped up something that was lying right inside the fence, a few feet from the grave. Even before he put it into his pocket, I saw what it was, and it was a case that eye doctors give people to carry their glasses in.

Then we dashed on behind the rest of the gang to the station wagon.

We got there just in time to hear a radio news commentator say, "The man is heavily armed and dangerous and may be disguised either as an Indian or a fisherman on vacation. The sheriff's office reports that he is restricted to wearing glasses while driving. It is thought that he may have abandoned his car, whose license number when last seen was Minnesota . . ."

All of us were crowded around the front

doors of the station wagon, listening. When the commentator said that, Poetry's elbow jabbed me in the ribs so hard it made me grunt, and I said, "Ouch!" and the rest of the gang said, "Keep still!"

My "Ouch!" and the gang's "Keep still!" smothered some of the announcer's other words so that when I heard him again he was saying, ". . . report to your local police at once." Then the news went on talking about something else, and Barry snapped off the radio.

Right away there was a bedlam of Sugar Creek Gang voices starting to tell Barry different things we had just seen that afternoon.

First, we told about the spooky-looking Indian who had come to the longest grave house in the cemetery and stuffed something through the grave opening. We all got interrupted by Dragonfly, who exclaimed, "Look, everybody! There he is now—that Indian! He—he—he's sneaking back to the grave again!"

I looked toward the pine tree away at the end of the cemetery, and there as plain as day was that same Indian, creeping along under the branches of the old pine tree to the front of the grave house.

Every one of us kept as still as mice and watched. Once, when I let my eyes stray to Barry's tanned face, I thought I saw an odd look on it, and I couldn't tell whether he was scared or not.

The Indian crawled back to the low fence,

stepped over, straightened up, looked all around, shaded his eyes, and with the little Indian basket in one hand, raised both arms up toward the top of the pine tree as though he had an offering to make to some kind of a spirit. Then he stopped, as if he had seen us for the first time. The next minute he was taking long, slow strides straight toward where we were.

6

While the Indian was swinging along toward our station wagon, I was halfway between being scared and being surprised. I guess I was *both* scared and surprised and also worried. I noticed that he had a broad grin on his face, and he certainly didn't look like the pictures of any of the fierce Indian warriors I'd seen in books. Except for his hair, he looked just like anybody else.

When he got close to where we were parked at the side of the road, he reached up a brown hand, caught hold of his long black hair with the feather stuck through it, and with a quick movement swept it off his head just the way a boy of the Sugar Creek Gang swishes off his cap. I knew right away that the long hair was a wig. His real hair was short like ours, and his big white-toothed grin had something very familiar about it, as if I'd seen him before.

And right away I knew I had, because Little Tom Till let out a glad yelp and said, "It's Eagle Eye!"

And it was! It was the big brother of the great little Indian boy we'd met up here last year, whose name was Snow-in-the-Face. All of a sudden I remembered that Snow-in-the-Face had been very sick and that we hadn't been to see him yet. Also I remembered that last year Poetry and Dragonfly and I had borrowed Eagle Eye's boat very early one morning to go fishing, and our little outboard motor hadn't been powerful enough to push the boat through the big waves that we accidentally got ourselves into, and we had had an upset. If we hadn't had our life vests on, we'd have drowned, maybe.

Well, it didn't feel very good to have half of our mystery spoiled for us. We found out that Barry and Eagle Eye had made it up between them that Eagle Eye was to put on a wig and do what he had done, just to give us an adventure in that Indian cemetery.

I say *half* of our mystery was explained right away, but we still had the other half left about the man in the white boat who had stopped at the medicine man's grave house. We all knew from last year that Eagle Eye was a Christian and didn't believe in leaving food and things at any of his dead relatives' graves. He knew what all the boys of the Sugar Creek Gang knew who listened to Sylvia's dad preach—and that was that when a Christian dies, he goes straight and quick to heaven to be with Jesus. He doesn't stay around his graveyard at all.

Part of one of the verses that Sylvia's dad quotes to us to prove that is "Absent from the body and . . . at home with the Lord," which means that dying is the same as leaving your body here on earth and going straight to heaven where Jesus is. I'd heard a lot of sermons about that, and that's why I didn't believe in ghosts in cemeteries or abandoned houses.

Even while Eagle Eye and Barry and the gang walked around quietly among the grave houses, and while Eagle Eye was explaining a lot of the Indian customs to us, I kept thinking about the white boat and the strange man and also the glasses case Poetry had in his pocket right that second, which none of the rest of the gang knew about.

Also I kept thinking about what we'd heard on the radio—that you're supposed to report any suspicious-looking persons to the police or the sheriff or the FBI right away. I knew that pretty soon the other half of our mystery would be spoiled for us too. For some reason I hated to have the police know about it, because I hoped maybe some of the gang could have a lot of dangerous fun catching the kidnapper ourselves.

But I knew also that it would be silly not to tell the police about any clues we might have. Police are smart, and any person who tries to be a thief or a murderer or any kind of a bad man is just plumb crazy. And even if he *could* get by with being wicked for a while here on this earth, he'd have to face God in the judgment after he died.

We were near the medicine man's grave when I was thinking about that, and Eagle Eye was explaining how glad he was, now that he was a Christian, that he believed the Bible about heaven.

Then he got a sad look on his face as he said, "But all my people don't know about the Lord Jesus Christ. Many who have heard about Him do not believe in Him and are still bound by superstition. My people are a very fine and wonderful people, and I have given myself to the Lord to try to win as many of them as I can to Christ."

Poetry and I were standing near each other, and the rest of us were listening respectfully to Eagle Eye as he told about Indian funeral rites, which are very interesting. All the time I was looking at the opening in the medicine man's grave and wondering different things.

Almost any second now, I thought, maybe some of the gang wouldn't be able to keep still any longer and would start telling about the other man who had come here between Eagle Eye's two visits.

Eagle Eye was explaining that, if an Indian funeral was held in cold weather, one of the members of the family would come in the evening for three evenings and start a little fire in front of the grave house to keep the spirit from getting cold on his journey to the spirit world.

It was Little Jim who piped up and said, "But they don't get cold in heaven, do they?" and Eagle Eye, who had been studying in a Bible school in Minneapolis, said, "No, but many of my people up here don't know that."

Then Little Jim said, "Do any people who *aren't* Indians sometimes come to the grave houses and bring offerings of food or things?"

Then I knew it was time to tell what we all knew. So we all started in, and each one of us squeezed in his words wherever he could find a place to squeeze them in between the hundreds of excited words of the rest of us.

In only a little while we were through, and Poetry had given Barry the glasses case and the piece of broken glass he'd found, and the broken piece of lens exactly fit part of a lens that was still fastened into the glasses frame.

We looked into the grave house and saw only a few dozen reddish, smooth-skinned Juneberries, which grow on a lot of small shrubs and trees up here in the forest. They were what Eagle Eye had pushed into the hole half an hour before.

Pretty soon the afternoon's adventure in the cemetery was over. We didn't know there was going to be an even more exciting one later on. We'd had a lot of fun and had learned a lot of things about Indians. Also some of the things we had learned from the Bible seemed even more wonderful than they had before.

After we'd all told about the man in the white boat with the fishing tackle box, we drove as fast as we could to the fire warden's house, which was between where we were and our camp. There Barry phoned the police about what we'd seen, and we knew that some of the smartest men in the North would pretty soon be watching all the lakes and all the resorts in our territory for a man in a white boat with a new tackle box and a large battered gasoline can.

Pretty soon the man would be caught—maybe that very night, although nearly half the boats up here were white! Poetry and I were alone for a minute after we got back to camp, and we talked it over.

Almost right away it was time to go on the fishing trip with Barry, who was going to use the new minnows we'd bought for him earlier in the afternoon. It was almost two hours to sundown, and just before sundown would be the very best time to fish.

I was still feeling a little sad, though, and I said to Poetry, who was doing something to his fishing tackle, "It hardly seems fair that we didn't catch the kidnapper ourselves, when we could have done it as easy as pie."

He was winding a new nylon line onto his reel. "Detectives and police have to work together," he said and grinned as though he wasn't worried a bit.

"That's a pretty line you have there. What test is it?"

"Oh, about fifty or a hundred pounds," Poetry said proudly. "In fact, you can't break it, it's so strong. We could almost make a swing out of it like we do out of ropes down home at Sugar Creek."

We were sitting on a log not more than fifteen feet from the Indian kitchen we'd made when we pitched camp the afternoon before. Big Jim and Circus were laying sticks of wood in place, getting it ready for cooking supper, which we'd have to cook quick so that we could get going right afterward.

Away over on the other side of the Indian kitchen, I could see Barry with his fishing rod, walking back and forth, back and forth between two trees and winding up his line.

"What's he doing that for?" Tom Till wanted to know, and Circus said, "He's winding up his dry line."

"How'd it get unwound?"

"Goof!" Circus said. "Any good fisherman always unwinds his line just as soon as he comes in from fishing so the line'll dry. If you leave your wet line on your spool, it'll rot, and then sometime when you get a big fish on, it'll break and your fish'll get away."

I looked at Poetry's yellowish new nylon line and wished I had one that was strong enough to catch a one-hundred-pound fish, if there was such a big one in any of the lakes up there.

When Barry had his line wound up, we watched and also helped him put a new sheer pin in his outboard motor.

After a while we were ready for our hurry-up supper, which was fried eggs and bacon. We used paper plates instead of our tin plates, because we didn't want a lot of dishes to wash when we were in a hurry to get started fishing.

At the dock our two boats were waiting. Besides Barry's two dozen chubs, we had two other pails with smaller minnows in them, which were called shiners and were good for catching crappies, the kind of fish most of us were going to fish for.

One of the boats belonged to Eagle Eye, who was going along with us to show us just where to catch the biggest crappies.

Dragonfly, Little Jim, Poetry, and I went with Eagle Eye. Eagle Eye himself was running the motorboat. Barry took Little Tom Till and Circus and Big Jim in his boat and came along behind us, following the widening V-shaped path our boat made as we plowed our way up the crooked woodsy shoreline.

It certainly was fun to go *put-puttety-sizzle* along on the water like that, and it felt good to sit where I sat, in the prow, riding backwards, with the cool early evening breeze blowing against my hot neck and flapping my shirt sleeves and with drops of spray splashing up against me.

I liked to watch Eagle Eye's bronze face, with its very high cheekbones, and the big reddish-brown muscles of his arms, which made me wish I was as strong and as big as he was. When he moved his arms, which were bare up to just above his biceps, I imagined that the bulging muscles looked like snakes wiggling under the skin.

On the way, Eagle Eye told us different things about the Indians of this part of the country. "There are eleven thousand of our tribe up here," he told us, which was ten times as many people as lived in Sugar Creek and was a *lot* of people.

Pretty soon, after a mile or so, we came to a place called The Narrows, and Eagle Eye said, "We're in the Mississippi now. This'll take us into another lake."

Poetry looked at me, and I at him, and we knew from the direction we'd been coming that this was the same route the kidnapper had taken when he'd gone to the lake where the cemetery was.

7

It was certainly an interesting ride. Our boat glided along in The Narrows. Sometimes tall weeds were on either side, and sometimes there were just shores with all kinds of trees growing on the riverbanks. All the time I was thinking about the mystery and the man with the newish tackle box.

Also all the time, Eagle Eye was telling us things about his people. This month, August, was the month when the wild rice up here turns yellow and looks like the golden wheat fields in other parts of the United States. Indians gathered the rice from the rice lakes just as they used to gather it almost three hundred years ago when an exploring Franciscan, Father Louis Hennepin, first came up here in 1680. The men still stood up in the bows of the canoes and with long poles poled their way into the rice lakes. In the stern of each canoe would sit an Indian woman.

Eagle Eye went on to tell how each woman would very gently reach out and press the tall rice sheaves between flails, which she had in her hands, and knock the ripened rice heads off the stalks into a basket or a piece of canvas in the bottom of the canoe. "Any rice that is left in the lake, sinks to the bottom to take root and grow for next year's *mah-no-men,*" Eagle Eye explained.

"What's *mah-no-men?*" Little Jim wanted to know.

Eagle Eye said, "That's the Chippewa name for wild rice."

And Little Jim, who's studied the Bible a lot, said, "Sounds like *manna,* the kind of food the people of the Old Testament used to eat, which God gave them from heaven every day."

"That's right," Eagle Eye said. "It does. Our people call wild rice *mah-no-men,* which means 'the great gift from the Spirit of Heaven.'"

Our boat putt-putted along with none of us saying anything for a while, only thinking. The other boat was behind us maybe a hundred feet, nosing its way along as the rest of the gang got their lines and hooks ready for the fishing we were going to do in that other lake.

I was also working on my line, getting it ready so that the very second we reached the place where our anchor would be let down, I'd have my hook in the water and ready to catch a whale of a big crappie.

All of a sudden Little Jim, who had had a faraway look in his eye—and who wasn't doing anything to get his line ready but was just sitting there with a dreamy expression on his smallish face—piped up and said, "I'll bet if Sylvia's dad was preaching a sermon to the Indians up here, he'd start out by telling them how much he liked wild rice—he'd probably eat some first—and how easy it is to digest or something. And then he'd tell them about the manna of the Bible, like he does us sometimes. And after that he'd tell them about how Somebody once called Himself the Bread that came down from heaven . . ."

Little Jim got interrupted just then by our coming out into an open place where we saw a bridge up ahead with maybe fifty people, Indians and white people, fishing from it. I didn't get to hear the rest of what Little Jim was thinking about and was going to say, but I knew it was important, because he had those kind of ideas nearly all the time.

Our boats slowed down while we went under the bridge, so that we wouldn't seem impolite to the people whose lines were hanging down in what is called the channel of the Mississippi. Some of the fishermen moved their lines to one side so our boats could get through.

Out in the other lake, Eagle Eye opened the throttle wide, and so did Barry behind us, and we roared out in the direction of what was going to be a very pretty sunset after a while, to a place where the hungry crappies would be waiting for us.

And then we were there. Eagle Eye shut off our motor and let our boat drift to a slow stop off a point of land that jutted out into the lake. We let down our anchor, and those of us in Eagle Eye's boat started fishing for the crappies he said were there, and which in only a short time we found out really were.

The guys in the other boat—Big Jim, Circus, Tom Till, and Barry—rode around in their boat farther up the lakeshore, where there was a sandy bottom, all of them doing what is called "trolling" for walleyes.

Boy oh boy! It was wonderful to catch a fish every few minutes and slip it into the net that we had tied to the side of the boat. Even Little Jim caught almost as many as I did, and also Dragonfly and Poetry. I caught not more than three more than each of the rest of them.

Time passed, and the sun went down and left the place in the sky where it had been the prettiest red-gold and purple I ever saw. The colors spread out over almost all the sky and made the water we were fishing in the same colors.

Suddenly I noticed that Little Jim was leaning a little against Eagle Eye, who was in the seat beside him, as though he was either tired or sleepy or else he liked that big bronze friendly Indian very much. Little Jim didn't have a big brother of his own to like, and maybe he was wishing he had one. He was looking up at the sky as I'd seen him do along Sugar Creek sometimes when he was thinking about something important and maybe getting ready to ask a question.

And because I wasn't getting any bites right that minute, I looked at the sky too.

Then I heard Little Jim say to Eagle Eye, "It's a pretty sky."

And Eagle Eye's voice answered, "The Great Spirit made it."

Then Little Jim said, "Is the Great Spirit the same as God?"

"There is only one true God," Eagle Eye said. "And He is everywhere."

I watched Little Jim watching the sky, and all of a sudden I had a feeling that maybe the thoughts that were in his mind were as pretty as the very pretty red and gold and purple sky that, because of its being reflected in the water, seemed to be all around us as well as above us.

"How come the Indians don't believe in Jesus?" Little Jim asked.

Eagle Eye right that minute got a terrific bite on his line and quickly landed a whopper of a crappie before answering. And this is what I heard him say, "Many do. But they are like anybody else—they have to hear about Him first."

Little Jim sighed as if he was wishing something important, which maybe he was. And right that second he got a whopper of a crappie on his line too, and you should have seen him come to life and land him in real Little Jim style.

Well, it was nearly dark, and we knew that on the shore it would be darker than it was on the lake.

Barry and the rest of the gang came around a bend just then with their motor roaring and came down toward us. We all got our lines out of the water, winding them onto our reels, and got ready to make the long motorboat ride back to camp.

"I'm hungry!" Dragonfly said.

And so said we all to each other. We wished we were already back in camp so we could have a bedtime snack. But we wouldn't get there as quick as we wanted, because Eagle Eye lived in a different direction from where we did, and he needed to get home right away.

Since there wasn't room enough in Barry's boat for all of us, Barry decided to let some of us stay at the bridge and fish if we wanted to. He would go as fast as he could through The Narrows and out into our own lake again and back to camp, get the station wagon, and drive back to the bridge and get the rest of us.

I say "us" because I had already made up my mind I wanted to try fishing from the bridge. If it got real dark before the station wagon came for us, we would use my pocket flashlight to bait our hooks.

It only took a minute or two to decide who was going to stay and wait for the station wagon, because different ones wanted to go in the boat. And a little later, Poetry, Dragonfly, Circus, and I were left alone to wait on the bridge.

It was fun fishing from the bridge with all the other people, some of whom were Indians. But after while, when Barry didn't come, we got tired of waiting.

Poetry said to me, "Maybe they had a flat tire or got stuck in the sand. Let's start walking up the road to meet them. We can't miss them, because that's the only road there is to here."

It sounded like a good idea.

But Circus stopped us by saying, "Maybe the station wagon had a flat tire right at the camp. If it did, they'll maybe come for us in the boat. We'd better wait a while longer."

"We could have hiked almost all the way to camp by now, if we'd started at the same time they did," I said.

Dragonfly yawned and said sleepily, as he and all of us reeled in our lines, winding them up clear to the ends of our rods, "I'm too tired to walk an inch. I'm so sleepy I could lie down right here and sleep forever."

"If you want to sleep forever," Poetry said mischievously, "better wait till we get to the Indian graveyard. The road goes past there, you know."

Say, did Dragonfly ever come to wide-awake life. "Indian graveyard!" he exclaimed so loud that two or three people near us jumped.

We finally decided not to wait any longer but to follow the lonely old sandy road back to camp. All the way to the Indian cemetery, we had trouble with Dragonfly, who made us let him carry the flashlight so that he could shine it on different things along the road to be sure there weren't any bears or a kidnapper or something else.

"What would a kidnapper want with a dragonfly?" Poetry asked him. "They only want people, not insects."

But it wasn't funny—at least not to Dragonfly. He didn't let his feelings get hurt, though, and was smart enough to think to say, "And who would be dumb enough to kidnap a lot of poetry?"

"That reminds me," Poetry said. "I haven't quoted a poem for a long time. When there's a pretty moon like that one up there, it'd be a good time to say:

"Hey, diddle, diddle, the cat and the fiddle,
The cow jumped over the moon;
The little dog laughed to see such sport,
And the dish ran away with the spoon."

Circus, who hadn't let out a bloodcurdling loon call for a long time must have been reminded of a loon because of "moon" and "spoon" rhyming with one another. All of a sudden he stopped in the road in front of me, straightened himself up with his face looking toward the moon, and let out a fierce, long, trembling wail that was so much like a loon that nobody could have told the difference.

"Stop!" Dragonfly burst out. He also said fiercely, "You'll wake up all the ghosts in the Indian cemetery!"

We were trudging along, half happy and half worried, wondering what had happened to the station wagon and the rest of the gang and Barry, when Poetry shushed us all from what we were saying and said, "It's right up ahead of us."

And it was. In the moonlight, those little grave houses looked very spooky. You couldn't see the one for the medicine man though, because it was in the shadows under the big pine tree.

We all stopped at the same time, I guess because we all must have heard something at the same time. I felt a tingling sensation up and down my spine, for I had heard something very strange.

We all huddled close to each other, and only our quick breathing and the sound of something out in the cemetery could be heard. The sound came from somewhere way at the other end, beyond the pine tree. In fact, it sounded as if it was coming from behind the sumac where we'd been hiding in the afternoon.

What on earth? I thought, and then I knew what the sound was. Somebody was sawing a board.

8

It's a strange feeling knowing you and three of your pals are alone on a sandy roadside at the edge of an Indian cemetery. And it's night, and the moonlight on the eerie-looking grave houses makes them look like somebody's farmyard full of chicken coops or dozens and dozens of extralarge beehives.

For just one minute while Circus, Poetry, Dragonfly, and I were standing in the dark shadow of an oak tree looking out on that moonlit cemetery, I was reminded of home. And right in the middle of my spooky feeling I was remembering my dad, who sometimes would have his straw hat on, with mosquito netting thrown over it and tucked into his leather jacket at the throat to keep the bees out, and wearing leather gloves to keep from getting his hands stung. He would be stooped over, using a smoker with bellows to squeeze little puffs of smoke into the hive and make the bees scatter in different directions, so he could get the honey.

And also even at that very second I got a sort of lonesome feeling for my folks. I thought about how Dad and Mom would maybe right that minute be sitting quietly out on the side porch of our house on our two red outdoor chairs that I had painted myself that very summer. Maybe they'd be talking about me being away up North. And Mom would be worrying out loud a little, the way she sometimes does. She does most of that kind of worrying at our house. And Dad would say, "Oh, don't worry about Bill! He's with Barry, and they have camp rules that won't let them be out at night where there's any danger."

Mom would believe him but would keep on worrying a little. And before they went to bed, Dad would maybe quote a verse from one of the psalms out of the Bible, and one or the other of them would pray out loud and name me by name.

Then they'd go in the house and stop in the moonlight that would be coming through the bedroom window and look down at my baby sister, Charlotte Ann, in her baby bed. And Dad would maybe give Mom a hug and say, "They're great kids—Bill and Charlotte Ann," as I'd overheard them say a hundred times. And Mom would maybe say, "Yes, but Bill—he's so impulsive, you know. He runs into all sorts of danger." I'd heard her say that maybe two hundred times.

That was as far as I got to think right then, because Poetry, who had hold of my arm, squeezed it so hard I almost yelled. My thoughts came quick from Sugar Creek, where they didn't have any business being at that dangerous minute, as Poetry whispered to all of us, "Who in the world would be sawing a board or something out here at night?"

Then the sawing stopped, and a hammer began to pound. And I knew it was a hammer driving in a nail.

I peered as hard as I could through the moonlight but couldn't see anybody.

Poetry surprised me by saying, "Let's go see who it is and what he is doing."

What? I thought. I certainly didn't have any intention of doing anything of the sort—not on your life. I said so.

"Then I'll have to go alone," Poetry said, and his husky whisper sounded fiercely brave.

Dragonfly whispered, "Somebody's got to s–s–stay h–h–here and stop the st–st–station w–w–w–wagon wh–wh–when it c–c–comes."

I could hear his teeth chattering with fright, and I quick shut my teeth tighter together so that nobody could hear mine, which had started doing the same thing.

Well, I don't know how we ever decided to do what we did, but we did. Dragonfly was too scared to go out to see what was going on, so Circus agreed to stay with him while Poetry and I sneaked around behind the pine tree to see what we could see. And you couldn't believe your eyes unless you'd seen it yourself, but as soon as we got to where we could see, there it was.

Poetry and I didn't dare whisper to each other about what we saw until we heard the pounding again. Then we went a little farther into the shadows and crawled along on our stomachs till we were closer. When I saw what was going on, I gasped with surprise, and Poetry did the same thing.

He whispered to me his absolute astonishment, and this is what his hot breath in my ear said: "It's an Indian building a new grave house. Some Indian maybe has died!"

I knew right away that Poetry was right, because there was a brand-new grave house, made of nice new boards and nearly finished. The Indian had a gasoline lantern sitting on the ground beside him.

"See!" Poetry's warm breath hissed into my ear again. "There's a shovel too. He's been digging the grave—no, it's already dug!"

It looked as if Poetry was right again. I felt very sorry for the Indian. I noticed, even in the gasoline lantern light, that he had a very bronze face and hands and that his jacket was like what I'd seen other Indians up there wear.

Just that second he straightened up and listened, and for a minute I thought he had a frightened look on his face. He glanced all around in different directions and, at just the wrong time, in our direction. For I suddenly lost my balance, and, in spite of everything I could do, I tumbled over on my side from behind the grave house where we'd been hiding.

The Indian held up the lantern and flashed it on me, right *ker-smack* into my face.

I don't know what I expected to happen right that second, but I knew that—if I'd been standing—I'd have been wobbly in the knees.

The tall Indian let out a moan as though he

was in pain and said, "White boy, don't be afraid. I build spirit house for papoose. We bury papoose tomorrow."

His voice sounded afraid and very sad at the same time.

"White boys go away. Leave Indian father alone with sorrow!" he said when he saw Poetry too.

Well, that was that—a very crazy *that*—but it made sense when we saw the hammer and saw and shovel and the pile of new earth and the little grave house nearly finished.

So Poetry and I scrambled awkwardly to our feet and started to leave. It was what Poetry started to do next that surprised me.

First, he said, "We are sorry, Mr. Indian, very sorry! We will go now."

But instead of going back toward the road, Poetry turned and started walking through the center of the cemetery. He had the flashlight and used it a few times, although here the moonlight was so bright that we didn't need it.

I noticed, though, that he was working his way over to the side next to the lake. Once he shot the light beam down toward the water real quick and then turned it off just as quick. *Then* he started doing the craziest thing, and it was then that I noticed that he'd brought his fishing pole along with him.

"What on earth!" I said to him.

"*Sh!* I'm going to dry out my line. Keep still!"

Poetry fastened the big fishhook that was

on the end of his leader to the limb of a sapling down about two feet above the ground. Then he adjusted the ratchet control of his reel so the line would unwind quietly, and we walked along, unwinding his new nylon line as we went. It was the most ridiculous thing I'd ever heard of.

Poor Indian daddy, I thought. *What if it was my father whose little Charlotte Ann had died, and he had had to dig the grave himself and get ready to bury her?*

A very sad feeling welled up in my throat, right beside the half-disgusted feeling I had toward Poetry for wanting to dry out his new nylon line at such a ridiculous time of night and in such a ridiculous place. Why, it wouldn't even get time to dry before the rest of the gang would be here in the station wagon. *What on earth!* I kept on thinking.

It certainly was a terribly long line, I thought, remembering that it had completely filled his big reel.

He let it unwind all the way back to where Circus and Dragonfly were waiting for us. When we got there, we stopped, and Poetry started back again, this time walking very fast, still unwinding as he went, leaving me to tell what we'd seen, which I started to do in an excited whisper.

"Wh–wh–wh–what's Poetry doing?" Dragonfly managed to stammer out.

I said, "He's going to dry out his line to keep it from rotting."

We could see Poetry moving along in and out of the shadows out there on the lake side of the cemetery. Then he would walk around *in* the cemetery, hurrying from one grave house to another and back again.

Then he came toward us fast and said, "There! I guess that'll tangle him up. If he tries to make a dive for the opening that goes down to the lake to his boat, he'll stumble on my line. And with all of us running wildly after him, he'll tumble head over heels down the hill, and we'll all land on top of him and catch him and tie him up and phone the police to come and get him."

"But he—he's an *Indian!*" I said. "He's digging a grave for his baby! He—"

"*Sh—sh!*" Poetry said when my whisper seemed too loud to him. "That's the same guy that was walking around out there this afternoon! The same one that bought the gasoline at the minnow place. And his boat is down there at the foot of the hill waiting for him to finish burying the ransom money where nobody in the world would ever think of looking for it."

"You're crazy!" I said to Poetry, maybe partly because I hadn't thought of it myself first, and wishing I had. Still, it didn't seem possible.

"He had brownish skin," I objected, "and he's got to be an Indian."

"He also had a brownish tackle box right behind him on the ground," Poetry said. "The same one he had this afternoon. He's probably got the money in that."

Well, it certainly was a tangled-up surprise. I wished like everything that Barry and Big Jim and the rest would hurry up and come quick, so we could maybe walk right out there with Barry's rifle and capture the kidnapper ourselves, if it really *was* him. Boy oh boy!

I was wondering, too, where the police were. Barry had phoned them from the fire warden's house a long time ago, and police are always on the job. There isn't a crook in the land that can keep on being a crook and not get caught sooner or later.

All of a mysterious sudden, I heard somebody's footsteps plodding along the sand road, coming from the direction we'd been expecting the station wagon. I shoved myself back into the shadows, hissing for Dragonfly, Circus, and Poetry to do the same thing, which they did.

Strange things were really going on around here tonight, I thought, when I saw that whoever this was was swinging something in his hand that looked like a basket or a pail.

It was Dragonfly who recognized who it was. "It's Big Jim!"

We hissed to him.

He stopped as though he'd been shot at, and when he found out it was us, he sneaked over into the shadows where we were.

"We ran out of gas back there, about halfway between here and the fire warden's cabin—" Big Jim started to say.

"B–but we just had the tank *filled* yesterday," Dragonfly said, and I remembered that we had, just before we'd driven into camp.

"I'll bet some gasoline thief must have siphoned it out while we were fishing," Circus said.

Well, it wasn't any time to try to figure out what had happened and why. It only took us a jiffy and a half to find out that Barry had stayed in the station wagon with Little Tom Till and Little Jim and had sent Big Jim back to the fire warden's house for gasoline. But there wasn't anybody at home. So Barry then had sent Big Jim on to the bridge, where we were supposed to be waiting, to tell us we'd have to walk partway home.

"What you carrying the can for, then?" Poetry wanted to know.

Big Jim said he thought maybe he'd be able to borrow some gas from some of the people who were fishing on the bridge, if any of them who had cars were still there. Or maybe some of the fishermen in boats might let him have a little, just enough to drive to town.

"I know where there is some—real close," Poetry whispered.

We quickly told Big Jim what we knew was going on in the cemetery and that there was maybe a whole five-gallon can of gasoline down there in the kidnapper's boat!

"That gasoline hasn't any business being in that boat," Big Jim said. His voice had the good old Big Jim ring of authority in it, which always made me feel good whenever we needed somebody to take charge of us.

I felt braver right away, because even though Poetry was maybe sometimes even braver than Big Jim, Poetry's bravery didn't have as much good sense mixed up with it. Besides, in a fight Poetry's fists couldn't sock half as hard as Big Jim's could.

We knew what we were going to do. We were going to sneak around the cemetery and down to the boat and set the five-gallon can of gas out in the bushes somewhere. We would also open the filler cap of the kidnapper's motor, and—if we could get the motor turned upside down—we would let all the gasoline in the tank spill out into the lake.

"But we ought to tell the police," I said to Big Jim, remembering what we'd heard on the radio that afternoon.

"Don't worry about the police," Big Jim said. "They know plenty, and they're on the job somewhere. Besides, we haven't any time now to get to a telephone. Hurry, before he gets his papoose's grave finished!"

9

Well, we were in for it—another whirlwind experience. And when I realized I was going to be right in the middle of it, with Big Jim as our leader to tell us what to do and what not to do—and with Circus with us, who was almost as strong as Big Jim—I felt wonderful inside.

We had to go closer to the Indian-looking man with the gasoline lantern and shovel, and we must have made more noise than we thought.

Anyway, he must have gotten scared, and suddenly Poetry gasped, "There he goes! He's making a dash to get to the boat before we do!"

It looked as if Poetry was right. I could see, as all of us stumbled along together and dodged through brush and trees to get to the boat ahead of the man, that he had grabbed up his lantern in one hand and his tackle box in the other. He was running through the cemetery, dodging the grave houses, and beating it for the edge of the hill that would lead down to his boat.

If he got there first, he'd shove off, start his powerful motor, and go *roarety-sizzle* out onto the lake. It'd be like looking for a needle in a haystack to try to find him unless you had a still faster motorboat. And even then, there'd maybe be a lot of other boats on the lake. And the Mississippi ran through most of the lakes, from one to another. Well, nobody'd find him tonight, anyway.

I didn't have time to think what would happen if something else happened, though. Right there in front of my eyes, I saw that dark form out there in the cemetery make a head-over-heels somersault. His gasoline lantern swung in a wide arc of white light and went *ker-wham* into the top of a grave house. There was an explosion and a blinding flash that was as bright as a terribly powerful photographer's flashbulb. And the next thing I knew there was a big ragged circle of fire in the middle of that cemetery.

"He's stumbled over my line!" Poetry said.

The guy must not have gotten hurt, because he rolled over and up onto his feet and dashed awkwardly for the brow of the hill and started down. There he must have struck some more of Poetry's line, for I heard him let out a string of swear words that didn't sound much like an Indian who couldn't talk plain English. And then he disappeared down the hillside.

"We've got to catch him!" Big Jim said. "Come on!"

All five of us broke out into the open and, like a football eleven, dashed wildly after him, being able to see better now in the light of the flames that were leaping up all around one of the grave houses.

At the top of the hill, I saw the kidnapper,

halfway down, unscrambling himself from what was probably a tangled-up somersault. He was on his feet again and starting on when he let out a terrible yell as though he'd gotten hurt in some way. He started swearing again like a cemetery afire, and it sounded as if he was not only hurt but was terribly mad at something or somebody.

One of us had a flashlight focused on him. He was sitting up with Poetry's fishing line in both hands and was pulling and straining to try to break it because he was tangled up in it. Even in the fleeting flash of the flashlight I saw that Poetry's hook was caught in the man's trouser leg. Maybe that was the reason he had yelled bloody murder a while ago—that hook probably was caught in his leg as well as in his trousers.

Poetry was just dumb enough and also mischievous enough to yell, "Look, you guys! I've got a big fish on my line!"

"All right!" Big Jim barked savagely. "Up with your hands! Quick!"

I guess I never had heard Big Jim's voice sound so fierce as it did right that minute. It sounded like a terribly authoritative policeman's voice.

The man gave a final fierce tug with both hands on that unbreakable nylon line. Then he shoved one hand into his pocket for something, which I guessed was a knife to cut the line.

Behind us, the light from the leaping

flames was getting brighter, and I knew we'd have to get that fire put out or we'd maybe have a whole forest fire. There hadn't been any rain up here for a long time.

But we couldn't afford to run any risk of what that guy might be going to pull out of his pocket, because it might be a gun. Quick as a flash, one of our gang, which I found out later was Circus, made a flying leap from beside me somewhere, like a fierce tiger leaping on an enemy wild animal. He crashed against that guy and bowled him over and scrambled on top of him, and nearly all the rest of us dived in to help.

The next thing I knew I had a bulldog hold on one of his legs, and no matter which way it moved or dragged me, I fiercely held on, feeling myself getting kicked in the chest and chin but holding on for dear life. I could hear myself grunting and feel myself happily mad and awfully glad to be in that kind of fight.

I knew that we were going to win and would pretty soon have the kidnapper under control. He'd have to go to jail, which wouldn't be even half enough punishment for anybody who would kidnap an innocent little girl, and scare her half to death, and do the same thing to her parents and all the people who had lived in their neighborhood back in St. Paul.

Even while I, with all the rest of the gang helping me, was capturing the big fierce man, there came into my mind a Bible verse that says, "Vengeance is Mine, I will repay." It sort of seemed that the Sugar Creek Gang was actually helping God catch a man who needed to be punished for his sins, and I was proud to be on God's side. In fact, there isn't any other side in all the world that's worth being on.

In less than several jiffies of grunting and straining and rolling around on that hillside, we had our man under control. Poetry's nylon line with the fishing hook stuck in the man's leg helped us to do it. While some of us held him down, Circus dived for the boat and with his knife cut off enough of the anchor rope to tie him up.

Then Big Jim said, "All right, gang. Off with your shirts! Soak them in the lake and get up there quick and put out that fire!" which we started to do in an awfully quick hurry.

"Hey!" Circus, who got to the lake first, yelled. "There's a fire extinguisher in the boat!"

Well, I won't have time to tell you about how we fought and put out that fire with our sopping-wet shirts, all of us working like mad until the last spark was out and there was only a lot of smoky moonlight, like bluish-gray fog, over that old Indian cemetery.

When the last spark was out, I wasn't a bit tired. In fact, I'd never felt so wonderful in my life.

The police still hadn't come, so we decided to get our prisoner up the hill and out to the road so he would be handy for the squad car when it came.

My bluish shirt certainly was a mess, being soppy wet and all black from the burned grass and also from being badly scorched from the fire I'd squished it onto again and again.

How to get the kidnapper up the hill was the question, when he was all tied up hand and foot. We certainly didn't want to carry him.

"He's still on the hook," Dragonfly said. "Let's untie his feet and let him walk and hold onto the line so he can't get away, just like a big dogfish!" which is what we decided to do.

Poetry managed to get his line untangled and all wound up again. He followed along behind, ready to keep a tight line if he had to. His hook was deep into some of the flesh of the man's right leg just above the knee.

We soon got him up to the road and made him sit down on the grass, where we tied him up again.

We certainly didn't have any trouble at all. He acted as though he was kind of faint. He just rolled over on his side when he got to the road at the edge of the cemetery and groaned.

He said, "My leg! Get that hook out. It's killing me!" Then he let loose a whole volley of swear words, enough to have come from five or six other guys as foulmouthed as he was. But all of a sudden he stopped right in the middle of his cursing, let out a muffled groan, and quit, like an outboard motor with its propeller caught in a tangle of weeds.

I hardly knew what had made him stop swearing until I came to myself and realized that *I* was the one that had stopped him by grabbing up my soaking wet shirt and pushing it *ker-slop* right into the kidnapper's face—which is what I wish I could do to most anybody's face when I hear him swear. It's such a filthy way to talk.

"OK," Poetry said. "Let's unhook my fish. Anybody got a pair of pliers?"

"Here's his tackle box," Circus said.

And I got a mysterious feeling again, remembering that some of the gang had said maybe the ransom money was in it.

Circus lifted the tackle box catch, opened it, and there I saw on the top tray a lot of new-looking lures: a green Jitterbug, a red-and-white Daredevil, a Kingfisher, a Jointed Pikie, a Hawaiian Wiggler, and two or three other kinds of fancy lures, which my dad used to say are put on the sporting goods shelves for the fishermen to bite on.

There was a pair of pliers in the top tray too.

On the second tray, I saw in the light of Big Jim's powerful flashlight some other newish tackle, such as a River Runt, a Shannon spinner, and other stuff.

But in the bottom, where I was hoping we'd see the ransom money that the daddy of the little Ostberg girl had paid the kidnapper, there wasn't a thing but air. I got a very letdown feeling.

"Give me the pliers," Big Jim said, and we watched him perform an operation on the kidnapper's trousers, cutting a little slit with his knife so he could get at the hook.

"Be careful," the kidnapper groaned.

And Big Jim was just as careful as he would have been if it had been one of the gang. "Here's why we have pliers on the roll call when you take a fishing trip," Big Jim explained to us.

He took those pliers, which had a place on them for cutting wire, and quick snipped the hook off just above the hook's eye. As easy as pulling out a needle, it just slipped it out.

"Anybody got any first aid stuff? Look in the tackle box."

Circus looked, and there wasn't any.

"Which," Big Jim said, "is something else we have to add to our roll call as standard equipment for a boating or fishing trip—a first aid kit."

Well, that's the end of this story, and also almost the beginning of another, because even though we'd caught the kidnapper, the ransom money still wasn't found—and *somebody* ought to find it. We knew it had to be somewhere. I had a notion the money was buried in the "papoose" grave—but when the police came a little later and dug all around, it wasn't there at all.

Poetry and I talked about it the next day when we were by ourselves on the dock again with our lines out and our frisky chubs down in the water, making our bobbers on the lake's quiet face look as if they were alive.

"I wonder where he *did* hide it," I said.

Poetry gave a short friendly tug on his line to sort of remind his minnow to come to life down there in the water and be a little more active. Then he answered between chews on some bubble gum and said, "I don't know."

"We'll have to read the newspapers to get any more news about him, I s'pose, now that he's really caught and has been taken to jail."

The rest of the gang were making noisy campers' noise in and around our tents near the station wagon.

Poetry sighed. "I'll bet the rest of our vacation'll be as dead as Sugar Creek after the circus has left town."

"Why?" I said.

And he said, "Because nothing could possibly happen that would be as exciting or as interesting as what has already happened in our first two days."

"Oh, I don't know," I said. "Something interesting *could* happen."

Just that second I heard a motorboat coming from up the lake somewhere, and I looked up to see that it was the big launch that always came this time of the day to bring our mail.

We had to pull in our lines, which we started to do, and Poetry, being in a lazy mood, started to quote one of his poems, making its rhythm keep in time to the turns of the lazy winding of his reel, as he mumbled:

"Sailing, sailing over the bounding main,
For many a stormy wind shall blow
E'er Jack comes home again . . ."

It felt good to think maybe there'd be a letter from home. It also felt good just to look far out over the water, away past the launch that was bringing the mail, to a very pretty tree-covered island about a mile away.

All of a sudden I got the idea that I wanted to be Robinson Crusoe and explore that island! The idea hit me like lightning striking a big maple tree down along Sugar Creek.

"That's what I want!" I exclaimed excitedly. "Hurrah!"

Poetry came to half-interested life and said, "*What's* what you want?"

And I said, "I want to play Robinson Crusoe and explore that island and find buried treasure and . . ."

That's how I began to think we still might find the ransom money ourselves. And that's the beginning of another thrilling story I'll tell you about just as quick as I can possibly find time to dive into it.

Boy oh boy oh boy oh boy!

Moody Press, a ministry of the Moody Bible Institute,
is designed for education, evangelization, and edification.
If we may assist you in knowing more about Christ
and the Christian life, please write us without obligation:
Moody Press, c/o MLM, Chicago, Illinois 60610.